Tom Goes to Nursery

Margaret Wild

David Legge

For Teresa and Zoran
M.W.
For Callum
D.L.

SOUTHWOOD BOOKS
4 Southwood Lawn Road
London N6 5SF

First published in Australia in 1999 by ABC Books for the
AUSTRALIAN BROADCASTING CORPORATION
GPO Box 9994 Sydney NSW 2001

This edition published in the UK
by Southwood Books, 2000

A CIP catalogue record for this book is available
from the British Library.
ISBN 1 903207 04 5

The illustrations were painted with watercolours.
Set in 23/35 Bembo
Designed and typeset by Monkeyfish
Colour separations by Hi Tech, Melbourne
Printed in Hong Kong by Quality Printng

2 4 5 3 1

Every day Tom and his mother and Baby walked past
the nursery school on the way to the shops.

'That'll be you soon, Tom,'
his mother said.

Tom thought: 'Yes! That's me building
a rocket! That's me being a king!
That's me making a monster!'

When they got home, Tom wanted his
mother to be an astronaut or a princess
or a googly monster. But, first, she had
nappies to hang up, clothes to put away
and dishes to wash.

So Tom was the googly monster,
and he dressed Baby up as a princess.

When his father came home from work, Tom jumped on him and said, 'Let's play rocketships!'

But his father said, 'In a minute,' because, first, he had to put out the rubbish, help cook the dinner and iron some shirts.

So Tom was an astronaut, and Baby was a creature from outer space.

And then — at long last — it was time for Tom to start nursery school.

'Yes!'

said Tom.

The whole family went to
the nursery. Tom pushed
open the gate, leapt up the steps — and
there waiting for him was Mrs Polar Bear.

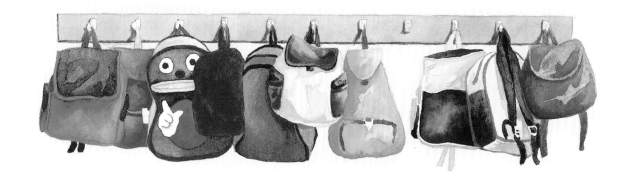

Mrs Polar Bear showed Tom
where to put his bag, and she
found him two new friends.

Tom hugged his father, kissed his
mother three times, then hugged
his father again.

'Have a good time, Tom,'
said his father.

'I'll come and fetch you later this
afternoon,' said his mother.

Suddenly, Tom didn't want them to
leave. He grabbed his father's left
leg and his mother's right leg,
and wouldn't let go.

Mrs Polar Bear said,
'If you like, Daddy Bear
and Mummy Bear, you
can stay for today.'

'Er, well, um ...'
said Tom's mother.

'Um, well, er ...'
said Tom's father.

'Yes!' said Tom. 'Please.'

So his father and mother and Baby stayed for the day.

They played in the sandpit,

and in the
dressing-up corner.

They painted a picture,

listened to a story,

and sang, 'I'm a little teapot, short and stout'.

In the afternoon, they raced home to put their paintings on the fridge. And when dinner was over, they turned the dining-room table into a castle.

'Do you like nursery, Tom?' asked his mother.

'I LOVE nursery!' said Tom.

'Me too,' said his father.

'And me,' said his mother, but she spoke so softly only Baby heard.

The next day at nursery, Tom hugged his father
goodbye, kissed his mother three times,
then hugged his father again.

'Goodbye, Daddy Bear and Mummy Bear
and Baby,' said Tom.

But they didn't
want to go.

'Don't you want to grab
my left leg?' asked Tom's father.

'Don't you want to grab
my right leg?'
asked Tom's mother.

'No,'
said Tom.

And he skipped away to see what
Mrs Polar Bear was doing.

Tom's father and mother and Baby

skipped after him.

'We're going to make sailor hats today,'
said Mrs Polar Bear. 'Won't that be fun!'

'Yes!'

said Tom.

'Yes!'

'Yes!'

said his father.

said his mother.

And they both hurried over to the dressing-up corner to find some baggy trousers and some sailor scarves.

'Don't you have to go to work?' asked Mrs Polar Bear.

'Er, well, um ...'
said Tom's mother.

'Um, well, er ...'
said Tom's father.

And they took off their baggy
trousers, and they took off
their sailor scarves.

'Goodbye Daddy Bear and
Mummy Bear and Baby,' said
Tom, feeling sorry.

Tom's mother went home and
mopped the kitchen floor and
washed the windows
and weeded the garden.

Tom's father went to the office
and signed a lot of papers and
made a lot of phone calls.

Then ... Tom's mother and Baby made a ship!
Baby was an excellent pirate.

And ... Tom's father closed the office door, made himself a sailor hat, sang a sailor song and —

hurried home to find out what Tom
had done at nursery that day.